Owen

Billionaire Blind Dates Prequel Novella

Toni Denise

For Kim, who always comes through when I need to name something or make a scene work. And who answers the car on long drives to help me work through these things!

Chapter One

Owen stepped into The Striped Keg bar and looked around. The dim lighting was a stark contrast to the well-lit street he had just come in from.

Men and women chatted throughout the room, most standing at tables with a few lining the bar. He came here specifically to avoid too much conversation. Plus, as it was across town, no one recognized him.

They could if they looked hard enough, but few ever did, and that was what he wanted. A drink and some peace.

Walking around the old wooden bar, he took a seat at the far end and waited for the bartender to notice him. It had been a disastrous week, one he'd like to forget, and here where he blended in, it helped.

"What can I get ya?" the bartender asked.

He handed over his card. "Start a tab. I have a ride home, didn't drive here. Scotch."

He always made it a point to let the bartender know he wasn't driving. It helped make sure he wasn't cut off before he was done for the night.

"All right." With a curt nod the bartender walked away.

"Excuse me?" A pretty blonde in a black dress approached him. "Are you Kyle?"

Owen shook his head.

"Damn. Mind if I sit here?" she asked as she set her small purse on the bar and sat down without waiting for an answer. "Why I let my sister set me up on some stupid blind date with a guy name Kyle of all things, I'll never know. Then he's not even here on time? Way to set the tone."

As much as he didn't want to be, he had to admit he was intrigued by the plain-speaking woman next to him. She didn't even seem to care if anyone was listening to her monologue, just kept on going.

The bartender brought Owen's drink over and turned to the woman.

"A beer, please. Whatever's on tap is fine."

"Add it to my tab," Owen said without thinking.

It was stupid. She was going to sit here now and keep talking to him and there went all hope for his night of peace.

"You don't have to do that," she told him as the bartender walked away.

"Looks like you could use a good break tonight, figured maybe it would cheer you up."

"I'm not going to sleep with you," she said boldly, causing Owen to choke on his first sip.

"What?"

"Just because you bought me a drink and my date didn't show, I'm not so grateful that I'll drop my panties for you tonight. I don't do one-night stands."

Owen couldn't hold back the bark of laughter that spilled out. "You're very blunt," he told her.

"No sense in not saying what you mean here in a dark bar with strangers. If you want, I can pay for my drink myself when he comes back with it."

"It's okay. I don't mind paying for it with nothing in return." He flashed his most charming smile at her. "I didn't intend to get anything for it as it was."

"Thank you."

Her drink showed up a moment later and he let the bartender know she was on his tab until he closed out.

"Why'd you think I was your date?"

"Wishful thinking, perhaps?" She shook her head at herself before turning back to him. "You were late getting here and your tie is the right color."

"My tie?" It was a light green, one he wore often, favoring the color.

"Yeah, he's supposed to be wearing a green tie. That's vague enough, but what shade of green? There's so many, and then so many men in here with green ties."

He nodded as he listened to her ramble on about ties. She was animated when she talked, and he found himself enjoying it and her company. Normally he carried the conversations but didn't feel the need to with her.

"Sorry," she said suddenly.

"For what?" He tilted his head, trying to figure out what happened.

"I always talk too much. It's a fault of mine and annoys people." She sipped her beer as though that was making it all better because she couldn't talk.

"Oddly enough, I was enjoying your speech on ties and the various colors of green."

"Liar," she said but then grinned up at him.

"I am in a position where I don't want to be the only one talking but I seem to always be doing just that. Having someone I don't need to pretend I want to do all the talking with is refreshing."

"Well, flattery will get you everywhere," she laughed. "Except my bed."

"Got it. Not sleeping together tonight."

She shook her head but laughed.

3

"Excuse me, are you Jenna?" A man in a poor-fitting suit stood next to her.

Still facing him, he could see the indecision on her face as she looked back at who had to be Kyle. He looked like a jerk and was definitely older than both of them.

Finally, she answered, "I am. Are you Kyle?"

He nodded and then didn't even bother to hide it as he checked her out from head to toe. "Must be my lucky night. You are stunning."

Owen rolled his eyes and sipped his scotch. This guy was going to get nowhere with her and he was interested in watching it happen.

"Sorry, if you were looking for a hookup, let me save you the time. I won't be sleeping with you for at least a few months, if you last that long."

Thank God he had already swallowed his drink or he would have choked on it again. Owen let a small smile sneak out as he watched Kyle try to decide what to say to that.

"Months?" Kyle asked, the shock evident on his face.

"At least three, maybe six," Jenna confirmed.

"Umm, well, I," Kyle stammered and pulled at his collar.

Taking pity on him, Owen jumped into the conversation. "Dude, just cut your losses and find a new bar and date."

Kyle seemed to just register his presence as his gaze slid to Owen. "I mean, it's not that we had to tonight, but like, that's a long time."

Owen just shook his head. "Go on."

Kyle seemed slightly relieved as he spun and disappeared into the crowded bar.

"You really should have let him sweat it out a bit longer."

"Couldn't. The man looked like he was going to pop before he ever managed a sentence."

"A pity he was only looking to get laid. I'm never letting my sister set me up again. Where'd she even meet him?"

Owen laughed. "He looks like a used car salesman, and not a very good one."

Jenna threw her head back and laughed. "God, yes. That's exactly it."

"Months, huh?' Owen arched an eyebrow at her.

"For him? Absolutely. If ever." She looked at her phone. "He's almost an hour late and was clearly checking me out before he decided if he wanted to have the date. It's going to be a no, bud."

"Bud?" Owen teased.

"He looks like he calls people bud."

He agreed and nodded. The man one hundred percent looked like he did. "Well, now that you have no date tonight, what are you going to do?"

"You're not my date?" Jenna fake pouted before giggling. "Don't look so horrified. I'm not trying to trap you."

"Not horrified, more curious," he answered simply. "So what was supposed to happen on this date?" Curious now, he found he wanted to keep the conversation going and know more about her.

"I assumed we'd chat over drinks and decide if we wanted a second date. Didn't really think about it that deep to be honest."

"What a crummy date," Owen said.

"I agree. I really should have just stayed home."

"Now, that I wouldn't have agreed with."

Just then Kyle walked by again. "Months," he muttered, shaking his head before turning into the crowd again.

"Dude's a creep," Owen observed. "Want to get out of here?" he asked her.

Jenna pinned him with a look that had him backpedaling.

"To get pizza. I swear. It's walking distance, too."

She stared at him for a moment, and he knew she was deciding whether to believe him or not before she nodded.

"Bartender!" Owen called. "I think we're ready to pay." So much for the tab he'd been planning to run up.

Chapter Two

S he was officially an idiot. Even if this guy, whose name she'd yet to ask for, was a good guy, she had left the bar with him and knew not the first thing about him.

"You okay?" he asked as they walked down the sidewalk.

"Yeah," she answered quickly.

"Really? This is the quietest you've been all night," he pointed out.

"I'm just trying to decide if I made a good decision or a bad one in leaving the bar with a stranger."

He stopped her by pulling her to the side in front of some restaurant windows. "My name is Owen," he told her. "The pizza place is two blocks that way." He pointed in the direction they had been walking. "Now, take out your phone and tell your sister she sucks for setting you up and that you're going to get pizza instead. The place is called Tony's."

When she didn't immediately move, he raised his eyebrows at her to urge her along. She pulled her purse to the front and dug out her phone, dialing her sister.

"Hey, you're a bitch," she said when her sister answered.

"He's not that bad," came Jessica's voice.

"Based on what?"

"Pretty sure he's not a serial killer." She could hear the shrug in her voice.

"I'm going to get pizza at this place called Tony's right up the street. Without Kyle. You are a terrible sister."

"Yeah, yeah. Have fun with pizza."

Jenna ended the call and looked back at Owen.

"Do you feel better now?" he asked.

Oddly, she did. It wasn't just the call, though that was part of it. It was more that he had practically made her call and tell someone where she was, to make her feel better, but she also suspected it was to make sure someone knew where she was.

"I do."

"Good." He started the walk again.

"So, Owen, tell me why you are being my date tonight instead of sitting back at the bar."

"You're more interesting," he said simply without turning to her.

Jenna looked around, wanting to look at him but deciding it could wait until they weren't walking. He was tall, much taller than her five foot three inches, which made him hard to observe as they walked.

"Here it is." He grinned and took her hand as he pulled her down a few steps and into a restaurant.

She held her breath as she looked around. Pizza place? Sure. This was like a place she'd been when she'd visited family in the Midwest. There were video games on one side and tables on the other. Families and couples occupied a few of the tables, and kids ran through the makeshift arcade.

The red carpet was worn, and the white tables were losing their finish due to wear. It was infinitely better than the bar, and she was already feeling better about tonight.

"Owen!" a large Italian man called from behind the register.

"Tony!" Owen called back.

"Take a seat wherever. Susan will be around in a few."

He led her to a table and took a seat across from her. Relaxed, she studied him. His tan was uneven and she wanted to know why. It wasn't fake as so many others she'd seen tonight.

His suit was cut specifically for him. It fit him like a glove and he wore it like a man that had power. Yet, he'd exerted very little over her except to make sure she checked in with her sister.

His dark hair was shaved on the sides but had some length to it on top. He hadn't shaved recently, evidenced by a thickening shadow of a beard.

"Like what you see?" he asked, arching a brow at her.

"Debating it," she teased, doing her best version of flirting.

"Well, what brings you in tonight?" A short woman in her early fifties walked up to the table.

"Susan, this is Jenna. Jenna, Susan," he introduced her.

"She's pretty. Doesn't seem stuck up. I like her," Susan said after studying her a moment.

Jenna grinned under the woman's praise. She suspected that this woman had judged other dates of Owen's and found them lacking.

He laughed at them both. "I'll have a soda and a large pie."

"Soda for me too," Jenna added. "Oh, what kind?"

"The special. You'll see." Susan winked at her before heading off to the kitchen.

"What's in the special?" she asked Owen.

"I've got to be honest. It's a little of everything, but it's really good." He paused and then took in a sharp breath. "You aren't allergic to anything, are you?"

"No, and I'm not too picky about pizza toppings, so all good."

Susan brought their drinks out and then headed back to the kitchen.

"Want to play some games?" he asked.

Jenna looked around and then nodded. "Let's go."

A few dollars in quarters stuffed in Owen's pockets after a stop at the machine and they were off. He pulled her over to a Skee-Ball game and dropped in the first few quarters.

"Do you know how to play?" he asked.

She debated playing coy for a second and asking him to teach her, but the competitive nature in her, and the fact that this wasn't a real date, had her nodding her head. "Loser pays for dinner."

Owen's grin split his face. "You're on."

He went first, scoring an impressive number of points. For her turn, she simply smiled at him before starting, knowing she could easily beat it.

She rolled each ball, and each time Owen's jaw dropped a little farther. She still had three turns left when she passed his score from his game.

"How?" he asked.

"Practiced a lot as a kid."

"Well, shit. I guess I should have been more specific when I asked if you knew how to play." He laughed.

"Sorry," she said without an ounce of apology.

"Come on." He took her hand and pulled her to another game. "Played this before?" he asked, stopping in front of a racing game.

She nodded. She was never great at these, but she had played.

"Good. New bet," he told her. "If I win, I get a kiss at the end of this date."

She turned to the game as though she were debating it as she tried to recover her nerves which had just gone crazy. "What do I get?"

"What do you want?" His voice had deepened as he stepped closer to her, touching his arm to hers.

"I don't know," she answered.

"Come on, think of something," he urged.

"A second date?" she said quietly.

"You're on," he told her and dropped the quarters in for both of them to play.

An intense game of Owen clearly winning and then wrecking and then somehow ending up back in the lead was over faster than she realized.

"Best two out of three?" Owen suggested.

"A different game?" She smirked.

"Fine. Two more." Owen stood and pulled her to another game.

Overall, they played almost every game in there except air hockey as there were kids on it. She had been in the lead on winning games as they went back to the table.

"Guess you're stuck with me for a second date." Owen pretended to sigh.

"I can't imagine how I'll manage that," she teased.

The pizza was delicious. Even the crust was flavorful. She'd be back even if it wasn't with Owen.

He paid and she caught that he had tipped an extra twenty before they stood up. Making a note of the kindness, she kept the thoughts to herself.

"Can I walk you home?" he asked.

She thought she was smart, safe, but her mouth had other plans, agreeing without her consent. She genuinely didn't think she had anything to fear, but a woman could never be too safe.

They stopped outside of her building and Owen let go of her hand. "Can I get your number?" he asked. "To set up your winning date, of course."

"Hand me your phone."

He unlocked it and handed it to her and she did the same for him, each of them plugging in their contact information. Then Owen surprised her. Turning away from her, he bent down so they were level and told her to smile, snapping a picture of the two of them.

"There, now you'll know who it is," he told her, handing her his phone back.

As if she would ever forget. "Thanks."

Before she could back out, she reached up and kissed him on his cheek before hurrying up the stairs to her building's door. He may not have started as her date, but the night had ended better than she could have dreamed.

Owen waited until she was safely inside the building before walking away. She definitely hadn't watched.

Once he was out of sight, she spun and leaned her head back on the wall. The smile was there to stay, and she couldn't have shaken it if she wanted to.

Chapter Three

J enna stared down at the magazine in her hand in shock. Her date had made the cover as the sexiest man alive and she couldn't quite wrap her head around it. Not only that, this man was a freaking billionaire. What was she supposed to do with that information?

He hadn't told her who he was, and neither of them had exchanged last names so it wasn't completely on him, but she wasn't hiding something that big. She had no magazine articles coming out about her.

It had been a week and she hadn't texted him or tossed out the magazine she had seen at the newsstand the next morning. No, she'd just read the article so much that she'd memorized the words.

She had no business going out with him. He was so far out of her league it was ridiculous.

Leaning back on the sofa, she sighed. She'd had such a great time though. Nothing he'd done except the extra tip had clued her in to anything like the man being a billionaire. Sexiest man alive wasn't a reach though.

At least she could confirm that he was single. The article had made a point of saying it.

I was Friday again now, and she regretted not texting him this week. Part of her wanted to go back to the bar and see if he was there. The sensible part of her said not to bother. Where could it possibly lead?

"I brought drinks!" Her sister, Brittany, let herself in the door.

"You are supposed to knock."

"Why? I brought gifts." She held up a heavy looking bag. "If I knock, you might not answer, and if you don't answer, then how am I supposed to find out what's been bothering you all week?"

"Maybe it's the terrible date you set me up on." Standing, she went to the kitchen with Brittany and pulled down glasses.

"Nope, I know better than that. You had a good time last week anyway. You told me as much on Friday and then suddenly you were miserable. So, naturally, I am going to ply you with alcohol until you tell me." Brittany moved easily through her small kitchen, preparing two mixed drinks and shoving one at her.

"I don't want to tonight. I'm not feeling it."

Brittany looked disappointed for a second and quickly pasted the smile back on. "Fine, then I'm staying and drinking and I'll just annoy you until you tell me."

Jenna groaned. That was exactly what she would do. She grabbed the drink and took a small sip before coughing.

"What the hell?" It was all liquor.

Brittany shrugged. "I didn't want it to take too long." She laughed and carried her drink to the living room. "Let's order food."

"Make yourself at home," Jenna muttered.

She loved her sister. She really did. They were two completely opposite people though, which meant that Brittany's bubbly personality was exhausting to Jenna most days.

However, they balanced each other out well. There were plenty of things that Jenna never would have done, good ones, if Brittany hadn't dragged her out to do them.

"What was that place you said you went last week?"

"Tony's," she answered.

"Was it good?"

"Amazing."

Brittany stared at her for a moment too long, and she knew her voice had been dreamy. The food was delicious but the experience was better than the pizza.

"Well, order it. Let's get comfy because I am dying to know what you aren't telling me."

"Britt," she started.

"Nope." She looked up at Jenna from the couch, a serious look on her face. "Look, I know something is bothering you. I just want to know what's going on."

Jenna sighed and sat next to her. When Brittany got serious, it was harder to shut her out than the party version of her.

"Let me order and I'll explain. I want a new drink, though, with appropriate amounts of alcohol for normal people."

Britt giggled and took her glass. "It's a waste of alcohol," she teased but made her a new drink.

Pizza ordered, she sat facing Brittany on her sofa and pulled out the magazine she had stuffed into the cushions before she showed up.

"I accidentally went on a date with him." She tossed the magazine at her.

Brittany picked it up and looked at the cover. "Shut up. This guy?"

Nodding, she reached to take it back. "He was at the bar and I mistook him for my date, and then he saved me from my real date." She pinned her with a look.

"You're joking. Are you sure this is the guy?" Brittany grabbed the magazine back and was flipping through, looking for the actual article. "He's hot!"

"Clearly." Jenna rolled her eyes; the headline pretty much said that.

"No, but really. What happened after?"

"Nothing. He walked me home, I kissed his cheek, and that was it."

"Wait, you're leaving a lot out."

Jenna retold the evening to her, including their bets from the games at Tony's. Brittany hadn't said a word the whole time until she got to the exchanging of phone numbers.

"He gave you his number? And took a pic? Show me."

Jenna pulled out her phone and showed her the pic that Owen had taken of the both of them and made his contact picture.

"You didn't text this man? Honestly, the whole date seems like a dream. Why would you let that go?" Brittany asked, still staring at the photo on Jenna's phone.

"I saw the magazine the next morning before I could text him. He's not someone I should even be pretending like it's going to work out with."

"Who cares if it goes nowhere? Live your best life and stop being such a worrying person. You had fun, go have more."

Jenna took a long sip of her drink. "Even if I wanted to, I didn't text him for a week. That's already a mess on my part that I made. He probably doesn't even remember."

"I doubt that. Let's find out."

Brittany stood and took off for the bathroom, closing herself in. It took Jenna entirely too long to remember that Brittany still had her phone in her hand.

"Wait!" She made it to the door just as Brittany turned the lock. Banging on the door, she yelled, "Brittany, please don't!"

"You'll thank me later." Brittany opened the door a moment later and handed Jenna the phone.

Quickly she pulled up her text messages to read what Brittany had sent. It was calm, thankfully, tame, and just testing the waters.

"He'll respond, just wait and see." The buzzer went off, letting them know someone was here. "I'll grab the pizza."

Brittany let herself out of the apartment to get the pizza as Jenna flopped down on the sofa. Now she was more anxious than before, waiting to see if he did reply. And then, if he did, what would he say?

Nervously, she stared down at her phone as she felt it vibrate. He had written back, and quickly at that.

Owen: Hey! I was getting worried you didn't want to hang out again.

Jenna: Sorry.

Owen: Don't be. It's been a long week.

Jenna: It really has.

Owen: So, are you cashing in on your winnings?

Jenna: Definitely.

Brittany was back and already eating a slice of pizza, moaning about how good it was as Jenna texted.

"What if he asks what I want to do?" she asked Brittany.

"Oh my God. How are we related? Just see what he says before you have a freaking panic attack."

Owen: Tomorrow night? I'll pick you up if you think you can trust me. This is our second date now.

Jenna: I think I can manage some trust. Where are we going?

Owen: Jeans and a T-shirt, be ready to have some fun. Location is a surprise.

Jenna: Okay. My sister has my location on her phone, just so you know.

Owen: Smart. I like it.

The conversation over, she looked up to see Brittany staring at her. "Did you just threaten that I knew where you would be?"

"It's a joke," she defended and took a bite of her slice of pizza.

"You are so weird. I'll forgive you, though, since you told me about this pizza place. It's the best I've ever had."

"High praise from a person that eats very little else."

Chapter Four

Owen had an idea for a date and had taken the time to set everything up, but the closer it got to time to pick Jenna up, the more nervous he was about his choice. She seemed to have fun playing games at Tony's, but now he wasn't sure if maybe that had been a fluke.

He was also worried she had seen the article about him. He hadn't told her who he was, but he hadn't lied. It had been too much fun to hang out and not worry about who each other was. There was no pressure on their accidental date.

For no pressure on the date, though, he'd been stressed about not hearing from her, worried he hadn't made the same impression on her that she had on him. Then he couldn't bring himself to text her.

He wasn't looking for a relationship. It wasn't what he wanted. He wanted his bachelor life and relationships just complicated things. But he craved seeing her again.

A mess, that was what his life was. All he knew was he wanted to hang out with her and if it didn't end in sex, that was fine, too. Was that more of a friendship then? He didn't know. His thoughts were complete chaos as the driver pulled up to her building.

The car wasn't necessary, but he didn't want to spend even part of the night concentrating on the road instead of her. Wasn't sure he'd be able to.

He texted her that he was there, and just a minute later, Jenna appeared at the top of the stairs. Standing next to the car, he opened the door for her to slide in.

"This is . . . unexpected," she said as he got in.

"I hope you don't mind?" he asked, worried he'd made the wrong decision.

She shook her head and looked at him. "So, this is casual you?"

"The suit didn't really seem like a good idea for what I had planned." He grinned back at her.

He'd carefully picked these dark-blue jeans and light-green T-shirt this morning. The green seemed fitting after it brought them together, and he couldn't resist it for tonight.

She grinned. "I like it. So, I'm here now. You going to tell me where we are going?"

Laughing, he shook his head. "It's still a surprise til we get there. I hope I made the right call, but I think you'll like it."

"Fine, be that way." She pretended to pout but couldn't quite hide her smile.

"Really, though, if you don't like it, you have to promise to tell me."

She studied him before nodding. "Do you think I won't?"

He debated answering her for a moment and then decided to just be honest. "I thought it was a great idea, but I'm not sure anymore. We didn't talk a lot about interests last week, and I realize I might be assuming too much."

"We didn't talk about much," she said.

"We've got a bit of a drive, no time like the present," Owen offered.

Jenna took a deep breath and let it out again. "I saw you," she said quietly. "In the magazine. The next morning."

"Shit," he swore under his breath. "I wasn't trying to hide anything from you. We just didn't talk about anything personal, other than your sexual preferences," he teased, trying to lighten the mood.

It worked as Jenna giggled. "I would never have said any of those things to you had I known who you were."

"I know." Owen nodded. That had been the whole point. "Is that why I didn't hear from you all week?"

Jenna nodded. "I nearly had a heart attack. Then I didn't know what to do or how to text you. I didn't text you last night," she admitted.

Owen arched a brow at her. "What?"

"My sister took my phone and sent the first message to make me make a move." Blush staining her cheeks, she ducked her head. "It worked out, but I was too nervous. I'm still nervous."

"Can we forget about the article?" he asked, hoping she'd say yes. He really liked it last week when she didn't know who he was.

"I'm trying," she said honestly.

"Tell me about you?"

"Well, I haven't been voted sexiest anything, so we can clear that up now," she said on a bubble of laughter. "Actually, that's not entirely true." More laughter.

"Do explain," he urged, curiosity having him leaning toward her.

"I write steamy romance novels. It's moderately successful. like, I am not as rich as you by any means, but I do own my apartment and I get by." She held her hand over her mouth as more laughter bubbled over. "Last year, one of my stories got voted sexiest cover of the month. So I guess I was voted sexiest something by proxy."

Jenna was crying with her giggling, and Owen found it impossible not to laugh with her.

"Well, I'll have to look you up," he teased.

"Oh, please don't!" Trying for seriousness while still giggling looked good on her. "I could not stand if you read them." She went beet red.

"I think I'd enjoy getting into that brain of yours for a little bit." And something else too.

"Nope, no way. New topic." She took a few deep breaths to curb her laughter. "Is this where we are going?" she asked.

"I hadn't even noticed we were pulling in." He nodded and stood when the driver opened the door for him.

"Laser tag?" she asked, stepping out.

"I assumed that since you were so competitive before that you might like it. If it's not a good idea, just say something. We can find something else to do."

The look of awe she gave him had him struggling not to fidget. "I'm gonna beat you so bad. Let's do this."

That was what he hoped. She took his hand and pulled him toward the building. He could see her wide smile in the reflection of the glass in front of them. This was going to be a blast.

They signed in at the front and were led to a room where they put on vests and grabbed their laser guns while getting instructions. He'd booked an hour for just them to play as long as they wanted.

Taking their spots on either side of the room, they waited for the buzzer to go off to enter the arena. The second it did, they were plunged into mostly darkness as they made their way through the hallway and into the arena.

Jenna got the first shot off and then couldn't hide for her laughter. He found her easily and took a few of his own.

Their laughter soon filled the arena as they ran around and looked for each other. He was enjoying himself more than he thought he would.

Cornering her, he snuck up from behind her as she looked out a fake window for him.

"Gotcha," he whispered.

With a squeal, she spun toward him. The joy on her face in the dim light was more than he could take.

Dropping his laser gun, he brought his hands to her face and covered her lips with his own. She froze but then melded into the kiss as her hands came up to his neck.

"You win," she said as she pulled away, her heart beating rapidly against his own. "I am officially incapacitated."

Chapter Five

As romantic dates went, this one was topping anything she could have dreamed. Even the women in her novels didn't get a guy like Owen, thought they might now. Or she might write it and keep it for herself.

When he'd asked her to come over, she had easily agreed. She wasn't ready for the night to be over either. She was also certain that if she put up a boundary, he would respect it, which went a long way to making her feel comfortable with him all the time.

His apartment was beautiful and massive. He'd given her a tour before excusing himself a moment ago. The deep colors that adorned everything were masculine but also cozy and warm.

A large brown leather sofa sat opposite a fireplace and television, but she was more interested in the view. Up high above everything, she could see the blur of lights below them and the chaos that was these busy streets. Not a sound made it through, unlike her apartment where sirens and car horns blasted all hours of the day.

It was a damn good thing she wasn't afraid of heights, she thought as she looked down. It really was amazing though. She could see the tops of the green trees in the park, places that seemed so very high when you were on the ground were now so very low.

"Sorry about that." Owen returned in sweatpants and a T-shirt.

"Damn," she said as she took him in.

The man did casual just as well as he did professional. It was a crime to look that good in sweats.

"Want to order something to eat?" he offered.

"Sure, whatever you have in mind is fine."

He nodded and punched something in on his phone before coming up to her. "I love this view," he said, setting his hands on her waist as he stood behind her.

"It's truly amazing," she agreed, leaning slightly into him.

They stood there for a few minutes, staring out at the night sky, before Owen stepped away. She immediately felt the loss before reminding herself not to get too attached. This was just going to be fun while it lasted. Unfortunately, she was already close to lost in him.

When she turned to see where he was going, she nearly ran into him. He had only stepped away, but not left.

"Sorry," she muttered as she took a step back.

Owen brought his hand to her jaw, tilting her head to look at him. "I swear I didn't invite you back here to do more than hang out, but if I don't kiss you, I will lose my mind with regret."

He gave her no chance to respond as his mouth came down on hers. She reacted immediately this time, opening her mouth and allowing his tongue to dance with hers.

From somewhere, a buzzer went off faintly. She nearly didn't register the noise over the blood pounding through her body at the kiss.

Owen stepped away. "That's dinner."

She nodded and then struggled to keep herself upright as he released her. A nervous giggle spring forward as she walked to the sofa, lowering her shaking legs down.

The man was like a drug. One that overwhelmed all of her senses and kissed like she had never been kissed before. Each time now, she had felt it all the way to her core.

She had joked that first night about how long she would wait to sleep with a date, but she really didn't have a rule. It was more that she felt Kyle checking her out and wanted to be rid of him, knowing that if she told him she wouldn't sleep with him, he'd walk away.

He returned with two bags of food, setting them on the coffee table before sitting next to her. "We have a few things to choose from here. I like it all, so you pick," he explained.

Jenna wasn't actually a bold person most of the time, at least not sexually. She spoke her mind sometimes, but that was more blunt than bold. But something in her took over.

"Okay," she answered.

Rising on one knee, she swung the other knee over his lap, straddling him. Unsure, she waited to catch Owen's gaze again before she kissed him.

His eyes were dark with passion as she looked down at Owen. It was all she needed to see to know she was on the right track.

With both hands, she pushed against his chest until he fell back against the sofa. Jenna leaning forward with him, she lowered her lips to his and took control of this kiss. He groaned as she did, and it made her feel powerful even as her body screamed for more.

In a flash, Owen cupped her ass and sat forward, coming to a stand with her legs wrapping around him.

His voice was raw as he spoke, carrying her. "I don't know where this is headed, but I do know that I want to see you in my bed."

She grinned against his neck as he carried her. They both knew where this was headed and she was more than fine with it. She needed it.

Gently, he lowered her to the bed, his arms still around her and her legs still wrapped at his waist. "Tell me you want this, too," he begged.

"God, yes," she answered, moving her hips against him.

"You're killing me," he growled out, backing away.

He tossed his shirt over his head and onto the floor as she watched, anticipating his next move. His abs were no disappointment, perfectly sculpted and as tan as the rest of him.

Pants next, he dropped them as she looked on, devouring every inch of flesh as he revealed it. His thumbs hooked the waistband of his boxers as he teased her, never pulling them down.

Jenna sat up and pulled her shirt up and over her head. Momentarily, she wished she were the type of person that wore sexy matching underwear. At least if it wasn't matching, it was good quality and not ones that had seen better days.

She left her bra on as she wiggled her hips out of her jeans, never taking her eyes off him. With one leg free, Owen slipped his boxers off.

"Oh my," she heard herself say and caught the grin Owen gave her.

Her bra was next, after getting the jeans off her ankle. His eyes roamed her body, leaving trails of gooseflesh everywhere he looked.

"You're gorgeous," he said in awe as he stepped away to the bedside table.

Condom in hand, he held his length as she peeled off her panties and tossed them to the side. She wanted to say something, anything, about how hot he was, but her mouth couldn't form the words as she watched him roll the condom on.

With it in place, he covered her body with his own and returned to kissing her as they both let their hands wander, exploring every inch of each other.

Jenna broke the kiss, gasping for air from his touch alone, turning her head to the side. The kisses resumed there, right in the hollow of her neck, and she let out a whimper as her body bucked beneath him.

She felt him nudge at her entrance and willed herself not to be greedy and lifted her hips. As he toyed with her there, just outside of giving her what she desperately needed, her patience wore thin and she raised her hips, feeling him slide inside.

Owen moaned as he finally pushed all the way in, one graceful movement that took her breath. She was going to die of sheer pleasure with the way he filled her, and it would be the best way to go.

Slowly he slid out before lifting away from her. Hooking her knees with his hands, he spread her wide open for him, watching her as he filled her once more.

He built up a rhythm steady, but faster and faster until Jenna felt her orgasm near. She closed her eyes and tossed her head back as she gripped the pillows, her body searching for the climax.

As though he read her mind, his hand came between them, finding her clit and stroking the nub twice before she came.

"Owen!" she screamed as she dove headfirst into the pleasure.

She felt him reach his own peak as he jerked inside of her on a growl. Collapsing onto her, he held her close and she stroked his back as they both finished their waves of ecstasy.

"You undo me," she whispered to him.

"Good, then we're even," he said, still catching his breath.

Chapter Six

Owen couldn't shake the thoughts of her from his head all week. He was distracted at work, to say the least, but when he was called on it, he finally gave in and went home.

Friday nights were poker nights with his friends and he'd missed a few recently due to hanging out with, or waiting to hang out with, Jenna. Tonight, he was sticking to his plan to hang out with them instead.

They'd chatted all week via text and a few video calls, but neither one of them had mentioned plans for this weekend. It was probably because it was his turn to plan something just based on what they'd been doing and he hadn't taken the initiative. She'd put a lot of thought into last week's date even if it wasn't as good as his laser tag.

That wasn't entirely true. He had thought of little else and had come up with a few ideas but couldn't bring himself to set things up. A relationship wasn't what he had planned on doing, and it seemed, somehow, that was where they'd ended up.

The sex last weekend had been amazing, but then she'd stayed the night and he was still shaken by it. He didn't do the cuddling thing, he didn't invite women to his place, and yet he'd broken both of those rules for her.

Well, not for her, necessarily. He'd been plenty selfish when doing both. He wanted her in his bed all night, couldn't have let her go if he tried. It had just felt right, but what did that even mean?

He'd also kept a really low profile about it with his friends, knowing they'd tear him apart over it.

As soon as it was acceptable to show up, he called a car to Jake's place. He wasn't going to drive, planning to have more than a few drinks.

The trip was short, especially for a Friday night, and he took that as a sign that this was where he was supposed to be, the right decision made.

"You're early," Jake told him as he walked in.

"I'm right on time," he pointed out.

"That's early. No one is ever on time." He had him there.

"I haven't been in a while. I am ready to take all the money tonight." Owen tried for a joking tone, but it sounded serious even to him.

"What's going on with you?" Jake passed him a beer and took a seat at the table already set up for poker.

Owen sighed and dropped into a seat as well. "I met this chick, on accident," he added as though he needed to let Jake know it wasn't on purpose. "Now I can't get her out of my mind. I spent the last few weekends doing shit with her, and I just can't shake her."

"She won't leave you alone?" Jake asked.

"Opposite. I'm thinking about her even when she's not messaging me. I don't want a relationship, man, but I don't know what to do." It felt damn good to talk about it for a change.

Jake looked at him like he had grown two heads. "Seems to me like you're already working your way toward one."

Owen nodded. That was what he thought too, just hadn't decided how he felt about it. "I'm here though, instead of with her."

"You try to get her out of your system yet?" Jake asked.

The odd thing was, he had slept with her, but it hadn't crossed his mind that doing so would get his mind off her. He nodded at Jake and answered, "That's the thing. I didn't do it with that intent and nothing changed."

"Damn," Jake said.

Owen's phone chimed.

Jenna: Hope you have a good time tonight.

He showed Jake.

"Is she being sarcastic?" Jake asked.

"That's the thing. I don't think she is. I know her and she'd not the type to send passive aggressive texts."

Owen: Thanks. I hope you have a good night, too.

Clicking his phone back off, he set it down. "I don't know what to do."

Cade and Evan arrived before Jake had a chance to reply. Quickly, he filled them in on his predicament. He had never intended to bring the night down with his shit, but once he started talking about it, he couldn't stop.

Cade whistled as Own finished his story. "You're sunk," he teased.

"Helpful," Owen replied, sarcasm heavy in his tone.

Jake had been quiet since everyone arrived but took the time to speak now, "The way I see it, you have to make a decision about what you want from your relationship with her. If it's just friends, you should tell her as soon as possible."

Owen sighed and ran a hand over his face. "Tell me something I don't know."

"I think you've already made up your mind and haven't admitted it to yourself yet," Jake added.

Owen groaned. That wasn't helpful either. He needed actual advice, not vague shit.

"We still playing?" Cade asked.

Evan had been shuffling the cards since he took a seat and started dealing without a word. Game underway, Owen did his best to push his thoughts away and concentrate on winning the hands.

Loss after loss, he pretended not to care. It was quickly becoming frustrating, but it seemed every gamble he took was working against him.

Angry, he stood and went to the fridge for another beer. His plan to get drunk wasn't working as this was only his second of the night. Distracting himself wasn't working either since he had to keep reminding himself not to think about her.

Jake joined him in the kitchen and stood quietly, hip resting on the counter, as Owen opened a beer and quickly tossed it back for a long swig.

"You know, if you just give into it, your life will probably get better," Jake told him.

"I don't know what you're talking about," he denied.

"Yes, you do. Don't play stupid ass games with me."

"Shut up. Let's go back to the game." Owen pushed past him to go back to the table.

Two hands and one beer later, Owen tossed his cards on the table, done with the game. "This is bullshit."

"No offense, man, but you're really bringing the game down, and we usually rely on Ryker for that."

Ryker was another member of the group but was noticeably absent tonight. "Where is he, anyway?" Owen asked, looking for any reason to change the subject.

"Out of town meetings," Evan answered.

They'd all worked hard to get where they were, and sometimes business called even if you didn't want it to. But they didn't all get to be billionaires by avoiding commitments when they were inconvenient.

"Sucks to be him. Anywhere good?" Owen asked. He reached for the hand he tossed to help straighten things up, only to knock over his beer, spilling it on the table and wetting the cards.

"Dude." Jake grabbed is attention and he scrambled to get the cards up. "Go get your girl."

Owen looked up and locked eyes with his friend, who met with him a grin. "Damn," he whispered.

Jake was right. He needed to realize that he'd already made up his mind and do something about it.

With renewed energy, he stood and slipped on his jacket. "Sorry," he said to his friends even as he headed out.

"He's a goner," he heard Cade say as the elevator closed.

Mind made up, Owen let the grin slide across his face. He was going to her place from here and tell her what he wanted, hoping she wanted the same.

Chapter Seven

"Come on, you'll have fun," Brittany urged.

She had shown up earlier to Jenna's apartment and caught her having a pity party about Owen not making plans with her for this weekend. Jenna had been obsessing over if sleeping with him was what ruined things or if she was being dramatic.

Dramatic was a funny thing to know you were being. She couldn't stop it but felt it nonetheless, and no matter what rational thought she had, it was always crushed by the dramatic one.

"Where again?" Jenna asked her sister.

"Brian's yacht. It would just be for the weekend, and we'd be back on Monday afternoon." Brittany took her hand and sat next to her. "I think you could use a chance to clear your head," she told her sincerely.

Jenna thought it over before agreeing. "You know what, why not?"

"Yay!" Brittany shouted, excited. "Go and pack, we are heading out shortly."

"In the dark?" Jenna asked. It wasn't dark yet, but with traffic on a Friday night, it wouldn't be a short drive.

"To the dock. We are setting out first thing in the morning, so the plan is to stay the night tonight."

Jenna nodded in understanding and went to her room to pack. It didn't take her long, and then she was back with Brittany in the living room.

"You're bringing your computer?" she said with a frown.

"Of course I am." Why wouldn't she? "If the mood hits me to write, then I'm going to do it."

"You're such a workaholic."

"And I am still going, so take it or leave it." Jenna put her hands on her hips and stared her sister down.

"No, please come. I just hope you take some time to actually relax."

"You know what? Fine, I'll leave it behind, but I'm bringing my notebook instead at least."

They headed right out after that. Jenna rode with Brittany, which was never a good idea, but she wasn't in the mood to drive. It meant that she was stuck until her sister wanted to leave though.

She took out her phone on the ride there and sent a message off to Owen, wishing him a good weekend. She meant it even if she was annoyed by it. After a bit, he wrote her back, wishing her the same, and that was all of it.

"Put it on do not disturb," Brittany told her.

Jenna looked up in question. "Why would I do that?"

"It's the best way to see what he's made of. Ignore him for a few days and see if he panics or goes with it."

Even as she scolded herself for listening to her sister, she did just that before slipping her phone into her purse. "Done."

"Yes, girl! We are going to have such a good time."

She'd been out with Brian, her sister's friend, once before and had a good time. Brian was a great guy and was absolutely in love with her sister who didn't see it.

Jenna minded her business when it came to the two of them. It was on Brian to work up the nerve to tell her sister how he felt, and if he didn't want to, that was his business.

They pulled up just as the sun was setting, and Brian met them in the parking lot. His broad shoulders and golden hair was an instant giveaway to his identity, even with his back to them at first.

Walking over the moment he saw them, he greeted them both.

"Thanks for having me," Jenna said as she took her bags out of the trunk.

"It's not a problem at all. Your sister is a little worried about you, so I hope this helps some."

Brittany elbowed him. "You aren't supposed to tell her I said that."

He offered her a sheepish smile. "Sorry."

"I don't know why she's scolding you about saying pretty much the same thing she said to get me here."

Brittany threw her hands up and walked away, her suitcase rolling loudly behind her.

Jenna and Brian shared a knowing smile as they followed behind her.

"What's the occasion?" she asked Brian.

"Closing a deal that has been months in the making," he told her before leaning down a bit to whisper. "And to spend some time with your sister."

"You should really say something to her," Jenna repeated, the same she always did when it came to Brian.

"It wouldn't be worth losing a friend over, and something like that would ruin a friendship if it wasn't mutual," was his constant response.

"Possibly, or it could be the start of something better."

Brian shrugged, signaling the end of the conversation.

They settled in easily and dinner was delicious. Brian catered to everything that her sister could possibly want before she could ask.

Dinner was seafood, not an odd choice for a yacht, but it was all

Brittany's favorites, something that Jenna couldn't help but notice. While her sister exclaimed over everything and how good it was, she didn't seem to notice that it was all prepared with her in mind.

"Drinks?" Brian asked.

"Yes, please," Brittany answered.

Jenna nodded, her mind working through the plot of her next romance novel based on Brian and Brittany. In her novel, though, her sister might figure things out a bit faster than she was currently.

They sat and chatted for a while over wine. She hadn't hung out with Brian in a bit and had forgotten how animated he was when telling a story. It was no wonder that he was in the entertainment business.

By the time the group went their separate ways for the night, Jenna had finally managed to put Owen from her mind for a few solid hours. She'd also not even bothered to get her phone out of her bag.

It wasn't until morning that she even realized she hadn't touched her phone. She had slept in, thanks to her phone being off, and the boat rocked beneath her as she lay there.

"Come on," Brittany urged.

"Give me a moment." Jenna shushed her.

She didn't have a hard time being out on the water, but apparently waking up to it was something different. She'd never been asleep when they left the dock.

Taking a few minutes to get her sea legs, she got dressed and finally reached in and took out her phone before going up to find Brian and Brittany. Breakfast was fruit and pancakes spread out across the table for them to build their own plates.

"Hey, sleepy head, nice of you to join us," Brian teased.

"I can't tell you the last time I slept this late," she replied, no hard feelings at the joke.

"I'm glad being out here is helping." Brittany squeezed her hand.

"I wasn't that bad." At least, she didn't think she was.

"Mm-hmm." Brittany rolled her eyes.

"I'll be back in a minute. I want to go look at the water and check my phone."

"You're going to regret checking it. Just leave it be til we get back," Brittany told her.

"I left it for all night, that's a big deal, and now I want to check my emails." And see if she had any messages from Owen.

"Sure." Brittany laughed but waved her off.

Jenna looked out across the water, enjoying the view as she waited for her phone to receive everything it had missed overnight. She leaned over the railing, phone in hand, as she received emails and texts.

A text from Owen popped up and she quickly brought the message up. She didn't have a chance to read it as her phone vibrated over and over as message after message come through.

"Everything okay?" Brittany said from right behind her.

Jenna jumped at her sister's voice, startled at how close she was. The phone fell in slow motion. It was as though she watched it fall down the side of the yacht and make the tiniest splash in the water.

"Oh, my God. I'm so sorry!" Brittany was right there on the rail, looking down with her. "I didn't mean to scare you."

Jenna sat down and looked out over the water. It didn't matter now. There was no getting it back.

"I'll replace it when we get back. I'm so sorry," Brittany was still saying.

"It's not your fault. It's mine. I shouldn't have been holding it over the water." There was no blaming anyone but herself.

"Do you want me to ask Brian to turn around?" she offered.

Jenna considered it and then shook her head. It would be easy enough to replace everything when she was back on land. All her data and pictures were saved to the cloud. She'd probably even be able to retrieve those messages.

At this point, she may as well enjoy the weekend instead. Brittany helped her to her feet and pulled her back to the table inside.

Quickly, she told Brian what she'd done, who also offered to turn around, and she turned him down as well.

"He messaged me." Jenna let a smile slid across her face.

"What did it say?" Brittany asked.

She giggled. "I didn't get to read them before my phone jumped off the boat."

"You want to use mine to message him?"

"Can't. I don't actually know his number. It was only in my phone."

She laughed full on now at the absurdity of it. She'd get it back when she got a new phone, but for now, she was without.

Chapter Eight

Owen was a wreck come Monday morning. He went to work and threw himself into it, locking himself in his office for the entire day.

There had been no word from Jenna since Friday night, despite the fact that she read his messages after that.

He wondered if he'd screwed everything up before he even had a chance to tell her that he wanted to turn what they had into a relationship. Or maybe that wasn't what she wanted and that was why she'd been ignoring him.

Jake was the only one he'd told. Very little help himself, he only offered to come hang out with him so he wouldn't be alone. Owen had turned him down, feeling more like being alone.

Today every contract got his undivided attention. His phone sat on his desk easily within view, but he pushed it out of his mind.

He'd caught a few things that he'd missed in contracts from last week and noted his team had already rectified them. Too distracted for three weeks, he worried what else he might have slipped through the cracks.

As a contract lawyer, he'd made his way up to starting a very successful firm and was disappointed in himself for not paying attention. It was a struggle to realize that he'd been less than his best.

By the end of the day, he wondered again at his decision. He was no better off than he was Friday night, completely unsure about what he wanted. Maybe they fact that he was getting this chance to realize everything was a sign that he was making the wrong decision.

As he put his computer to sleep for the night, he picked up his phone and decided he'd try one last time and called Jenna.

"Hey!" Jenna answered, breathless.

"Hey," Owen's tone was solemn.

"You aren't going to believe what happened to me this weekend."

"Oh?" Owen asked. He didn't really have a plan for if she answered, as he hadn't expected her to.

"I dropped my phone in the ocean Saturday morning," she told him.

"You what?" he asked in disbelief.

"Look, is there any chance you could meet me for dinner? I'd like to see you, and frankly, I know how lame that sounds, but I really, truly, just finished setting up my new phone."

"Tony's?" he offered.

"Sounds great. Meet you in an hour?"

"I'll be there."

It seemed fitting that he chose their first date as what could possibly be there last. She'd dropped her phone in the ocean? What did that even mean?

Owen took his time, straightening his office before he left. No matter what, he was going to be early.

Owen: She wants to meet tonight. Said she dropped her phone in the ocean Saturday morning.

Jake: Are you serious?

Owen: That's all she said then asked to meet.

Jake: You're meeting her, right?

Owen: At Tony's around seven. I'm on my way there.
Jake: I'm sure she's great, but don't fall for some bullshit.
Owen: I don't intend to.

He was early as he knew he would be, so he grabbed a table and waited, facing the door, waiting to see her walk in.

About quarter til, she did, and his stomach flipped as she looked around before finding him. A smile lit her face when she did, and she hurried over to him, a brown bag in her hand.

"I thought I was going to be early," she laughed.

"I was just leaving work when you answered." He was doing his best not to reach across the table and take her hand. He needed to hear what she had to say before he acted like a lovesick fool.

Jenna reached in the bag and pulled out a folded paper and slid it over to him. "I'm just coming from the phone store closest to the dock. I've literally been on the ocean all weekend and just got back."

He briefly looked down at the paper and slid it back to her. "I don't need you to account for anything."

"No, listen. I put my phone on do not disturb Friday night when my sister convinced me to go out with her and Brian on the yacht. I was a little upset that you hadn't planned a date this weekend and didn't know what that meant, if anything."

Owen opened his mouth to speak but she held up her palm.

"Let me, please? Saturday, without a phone alarm, I slept in. Then when my sister woke me up, I went outside and waited for my phone to download everything I had missed." She sighed. "I was leaning over the rail and my sister came up behind me as your messages came through. She scared me, on accident, and my phone went for a swim."

Owen leaned back in his chair and took it all in. It was too crazy not to be true, not that he thought she would lie to him.

"Are you okay otherwise?" he asked.

"I am. Full disclosure, they offered to turn the whole boat around for me after that happened, but I told them no. I regret that some, but

I didn't want to stop their getaway over a phone. I couldn't message you from anyone else's phone, though, because I didn't have your number anywhere but there, and my sister talked me out of bringing my computer," she rushed out.

"I thought you were mad at me," he told her.

"No!" She shook her head, her hair swinging as she did. "Had I read your messages, I might have let them turn around, but I thought that you were maybe over hanging out with me."

"We suck at communicating." Owen shook his head. "I was putting you off a little bit, trying to figure out if we were moving too fast, but then I changed my mind, and by the time I tried to tell you that, your phone must have been off."

"This is the type of shit I would create in a book, but I would maybe drag it out more than a weekend," she joked.

The pizza arrived and Owen quickly served them both a slice. He was thrilled it wasn't the disaster he was worried it would have been, or could have been, but he didn't know what to do next.

"I have a nine o'clock meeting with my agent in the morning on a new story I want to do, but I'd like to maybe see you tomorrow?" She bit her lip as she waited for his response.

Owen nodded. "I'd like that, too." It would give him some time to put his thoughts back together after they cleared things up.

"How about something different? I can cook something for us?" she offered.

She was inviting him over? He wondered at her choice with something so intimate but readily agreed. He wanted to see her place and know more about her. To see her in a place where she was most comfortable intrigued him.

"Thank you for meeting me tonight and hearing me out. And for not being a complete ass about it."

"There's no reason to be. It was a long weekend, but I think we both screwed up," he told her.

They parted ways after the conversation with a hug and a quick kiss goodnight. Though they had talked, the air between them had somehow changed and he didn't know why, or how, to fix it.

He had until tomorrow to figure it out. He went home and did the one thing he could think of to do.

Chapter Nine

J enna had pitched her idea to her agent this morning and it had gone surprisingly well. The story based on the kind of complicated relationship between Brian and Brittany was a go.

Then she'd gotten to the store, grabbed groceries, and started a pot roast in her crock pot. Once that was done, she'd clean the heck out of her apartment. It was far from dirty, but she'd done it anyway.

By evening, she had thoroughly scrubbed every inch of her apartment and was in the kitchen preparing sides and dessert for dinner. Owen had texted her earlier, confirming a time, and that was all she'd heard from him.

She didn't miss his small confession last night that he had been avoiding her Friday. It hurt a little to hear but he'd also admitted that he'd changed his mind. It left her reeling, and that was why she had ended dinner a little sooner that she planned.

The plan had been to try to play a few games and then see what happened. Instead, they'd only had the pizza and called it a night. It was a mess, if she admitted it.

Owen was due to arrive in half an hour and she was in a rush to get the rest of her sides completed. She was making everything from scratch and it took longer, but she knew cooking was a strength of hers, so she pushed forward because it would taste better than store bought.

Once everything was done, she set the table and put the pie in for dessert and waited for Owen to text or buzz that he was here. She went over everything again in her mind as she sat.

Tonight she was going to tell Owen what she wanted from their relationship, and she prayed he was on board. It was terrifying to think that he might not be, but she'd planned for that as well.

If he told her he wasn't interested, she was going to let him go. She couldn't be like Brian and just remain friends when she wanted more. It would hurt too much.

Owen texted when he got there, and she checked the pie before hurrying down the stairs to let him in. He was still in his suit from work and held a bouquet of roses out for her when she opened the door.

"Thank you." She blushed as she took them from him.

He stepped in and stood there awkwardly before she headed up the stairs. Owen followed but hadn't said a word, and she couldn't help but wonder, for the millionth time, if they had already lost whatever they had.

"It smells amazing, whatever it is," Owen said as she opened the door to her apartment.

"Thank you. I made a pot roast, mashed potatoes, brussel sprouts, and rolls. Oh, and there's an apple pie in the oven."

She hurried over to the counter and pulled out a vase, putting the flowers in. They were beautiful red roses and she couldn't stop herself from burying her nose in one of them and taking a deep breath.

"I'm glad you like them," Owen said.

"Sorry, I love the smell of fresh roses." She blushed and pushed them back on the counter. "Everything is ready so we can eat."

He nodded and went to her table, taking off his jacket and

draping it across the back of the chair before taking a seat. Quietly, she served the food for each of them and carried the plates to the table.

"This is better than it smells," he told her as he took a bite of the roast.

"I'm glad you like it. I wasn't sure if you would."

Owen set his fork down and looked at her. "This is awkward, huh?"

She wanted to say no but nodded. It was, and there was no way around it.

"Can I be honest with you?" he asked.

"Always, I hope," she answered, setting her own fork down to give him her full attention.

"I hate that it's awkward. I wanted to plan something big and grand, but everything felt corny. I don't mean anything by that. I just couldn't find something right for us."

She nodded.

"I don't know what we are doing, you and me, as far as this relationship goes, but I want to have one with you. I want to see where things lead between us. I want to know your phone number by heart, and you mine." He winked. "I don't want to wonder where we stand anymore, and I hope that you want that, too."

She gaped at him. That was pretty much what she had planned to say to him and was floored that he had done it first. She stood from her chair, walking around the table to where he was sitting.

"If you don't want to, that's fine, I'm not going to be mad, but—"

She cut him off as she covered his lips with hers. The words might not have come out right away, but that was what she wanted and needed him to know.

"I am falling in love with you," she whispered as she broke the kiss. "I was going to tell you tonight."

"Thank God." Owen pulled her down onto his lap, dinner forgotten, to deepen the kiss. "I love you," he told her.

As she stood, she couldn't help the giggle that slid out. "I memorized your phone number," she told him as she went back to her seat.

"I may have to test you on that later," he teased.

"Just to be sure," she agreed.

"Are we less awkward now?" he asked.

"Tremendously. Tell me the truth, though. How's dinner?"

"I have never had a roast this good."

"Flattery," she scoffed.

"I bet dessert will be even better," he said huskily, lust darkening his eyes and deepening his voice.

"There is pie," she said nervously.

"There is that, but I was thinking of something else," he said.

"A mid-dinner dessert?" she asked.

"I don't think I've ever had that course before. We could turn it into a trend," he joked as he stood and held out a hand for her.

"Or keep it a secret." She let him help her up and pressed her lips to his.

"Or that," he agreed, bending down and lifting her into his arms. "I love you," he told her as he held her.

"I love you, too." She smiled back at him.

THE END

Jake

First full length novel in the Billionaire Blind Dates Series

Five men form a bond over their mutual business opportunities and the trials of finding real love in a world of greed.

After Jake discovered his last girlfriend was in it only for his money, he has given up on dating, tired of being used. It's hard to find the right woman for him when everyone knows who he is and what's in his bank account. At poker night with his friends, they come up with a plan. They will all use the new blind date service offered in town where everything is done through an app and dinner dates are done in the dark with only minimal lighting to see if the pair hit things off. Each man gets to pick a person for the others to blind date, with just a few rules.

Lauren doesn't like rich men. Almost all the ones she's known seem to think that women should bow down to them since they have money. She's over it and would like to find a respectable man to date that doesn't have loads in the bank. Someone who, like her, just wants to live comfortably, not lavishly. She also hates being thrust into the media. When her boss's sister begs her to go on a blind date, she reluctantly agrees, thinking she will just get it over with to stop her from asking again.

Lauren and Jake hit things off immediately. How will Lauren react when she finds out who Jake is? How will Jake react when he finds out he's dating his friend's assistant?

Stay Tuned for a one chapter preview!

Jake Chapter 1

"Heard you and Celia broke up already," Cade said as he dealt cards at their weekly poker game.

"Shut up." Jake pulled off his tie with a yank and hung it over the back of his chair where it joined his blue suit jacket.

"Already?" Evan picked up his cards but looked at Jake.

"How do you even know?" Jake looked at his cards; his hand was crap, same as his love life lately.

"It was in the news. My sister told me," Cade answered as he looked at his own cards, his dark hair falling forward as he looked down.

Cade's sister, Catherine, was always in the know but was not a gossip about them. Her loyalty was everything to her and if you had it, she'd defend you forever. Cade Hawkins owned a successful marketing firm and Catherine did all their internal public relations. She'd helped all of them out at least once.

Jake blew out a breath and set his cards face down on the table. "There it is, as usual."

Every woman he seemed to think was going to be worth dating always wanted their names in the press. No doubt she had painted him as the bad one, no matter that it was Celia's demands for an engagement ring two weeks into their relationship that had caused him to break it off.

They all wanted his money and the status that came with it. Not a single one wanted to have a conversation unless it was about spending money, and he was so sick of it.

"What'd she do?" Evan scratched his chin and the stubble that he could never keep at bay. He shaved and still had a shadow right after.

"Surprised me by showing up at the office today with a selection of engagement rings for me to choose from for her." He'd nearly lost his mind on her but had managed to calmly ask her to leave and just told her they were through. She, on the other hand, threw a fit.

Ryker, usually silent, let out a long whistle and rocked back in his chair, lifting the front two legs off the ground. "I don't know why you keep trying to date these chicks. Too much hope." He rolled his sleeves up, preparing to play, showing his tattoos.

The elevator chimed and Luke exited, completing their group. "What'd I miss?" he asked as he let himself into Jake's kitchen, grabbing a beer from the fridge.

Luke was the youngest of them and couldn't grow a beard if he tried, and he had tried. They'd teased him relentlessly. With dark hair like most of the men there, Luke was also tan always, a benefit of his daily runs at the park.

"Help yourself," Jake called.

Luke grinned, by far the happiest of the group. "Of course." He took the last seat at the table. "You started without me?" he teased.

"You were late," Ryker grumped.

"I had a meeting I couldn't miss, you know, work?" Luke threw at him.

Jake leaned back in his chair and looked around as the banter at the table continued. He had a penthouse apartment, open floor plan, magnificent view, everything he was supposed to want, but something was still missing. He was tired of meaningless relationships and bullshit conversations.

His kitchen was directly in his view and he took a critical eye toward it. The stark white cabinets shined against his dark walls and stainless-steel appliances. The granite countertops had been a feat for him to get; the bar was one massive slab and had taken engineers to figure out how to get it up to this floor.

They'd managed it; money always saw the impossible managed. He rarely used the kitchen, though, as he was hardly ever home. No woman had cooked in it either. He held all dates far from his private sanctuary until he determined they were not looking for money or fame, and sadly, no one had met that bar yet.

"Earth to Jake," Evan called, pulling him from his musings.

He sat forward and picked up his cards. "Sorry, is it my turn?" He shuffled them, hoping for a better hand as he checked the cards on the table. After debating a few times, he sighed and said, "I fold."

They went around a few times and Ryker took the pot on the table. They all had more than enough money to lose to each other every hand, but they never bet real money. Ryker, who won more than anyone else, didn't gamble, and none of them had anything to gain by taking each other's money, so they played for chips and bragging rights.

"Deal me in, time to take him down," Luke added cheerfully.

"In your dreams, kid," Ryker threw at him.

Luke shifted in his seat. "You'll see."

Ryker had called Luke kid since they'd added him to their friend group a few years ago. There was little else that annoyed Luke as much as being called a kid and Ryker knew it.

"Knock it off," Cade told Ryker.

The four of them all turned toward Ryker, the only one that was sitting there in a black shirt. Ryker was the most quick-tempered of them, too. He hadn't even wanted to be a part of their group at first. Evan had managed it when Cade, Jake, and Evan were ready to abandon him.

Their group had been a bond that had helped them all manage the politics and financials of their growing companies. Every man at this table had a net worth now of over seven figures, and with that they only found additional problems.

"What about blind dates?" Evan offered Jake as the game continued.

Ryker snorted and Luke straight laughed.

"No, really, there's that new place now that does actual blind dates. You don't even get to see each other." Evan placed a bet after checking his cards.

"It's not a terrible idea," Cade said at his turn.

Jake raised an eyebrow in question. Of all the people to be on board with that, it wasn't Cade he would have suspected.

"See?" Evan smiled.

"It's the perfect solution to our problems." Cade shrugged. He was selling it but was far from enthusiastic about it.

"I'm not here for spectacles." Jake folded again.

"How can it be any worse that what you're going through right now?" Luke asked.

Jake looked to Ryker for help, who only shrugged. It seemed it was up to Jake to explain how ridiculous the idea was.

"What would happen the moment she sees my name? She'd look me up and we'd be right where I am now. No difference, just more hoops to jump through." He'd remembered reading about the blind date restaurant opening up but hadn't really looked into it.

Evan took the pot, and the game paused as he shuffled cards. "That's the beauty of the place. I'm considering investing in it." He started dealing. "They don't give any of your information to each other. You can elect to chat in their app before the date if you want, or you meet them in the dark at the restaurant and you get to decide when to reveal yourselves or to stop dating."

"You know entirely too much about this." Cade, like the rest of them, had been staring at Evan since he launched into the explanation.

Evan was unbothered by the scrutiny. "I told you I was thinking about investing in it. Regardless, it solves all the problems that Mr. Hottest Man of the Year is having."

Jake groaned. He couldn't wait until the magazine that had called him that came out again in six more months to give someone else that name. His life had gotten even crazier since then and the media never left him alone on a date.

"It has merit," Ryker added, looking over at Jake.

"Not you too?" Jake was growing more irritated. "Can we talk about something other than my love life?"

"Not that you have one," Cade muttered.

"Low blow," Luke scolded.

"How is Luke the only one on my side?" Jake stood, knocking the chair out from under him.

"He's still enjoying the meaningless sex," Cade answered for the group.

Jake ran a hand through his dark brown hair, messing its usually perfect style up. "Fine, if I agree to one date, can we just get back to the game?"

"Nope, one from each of us." Evan smiled.

"Four dates then?" Jake conceded.

"Plus any you choose through the app," Evan added again, still grinning.

"I can guarantee you that won't happen." Jake had no intention of looking through a dating app of any kind, not to mention one with even less information than the normal ones. "Four dates and then no one else butts in again with stupid suggestions."

"I'll set it all up. Men, email me your picks by end of next week."

They nodded as Jake picked his chair up, sliding it under the table and taking a seat. This was going to be interesting for sure.

Hours passed as their game dragged on. In the end, Ryker won, as usual. Luke's goal was to take Ryker down and he grew more frustrated every night that he didn't win. Although, he'd come close tonight.

Jake threw the last of the empty bottles away and wiped down the table before dropping onto his black leather sofa and propping his feet on the ottoman he'd argued with his interior designer about buying. She'd practically fainted when he refused a coffee table for this. He told her he meant to put his feet on it regardless and she'd finally given up.

Evan wasted no time and sent him the link for the app for the blind dates the second he'd agreed. He pulled it up and clicked to start the download. If he was really going to go through with it, he figured he might as well research it.

It took nearly an hour to put all his information in and take the million-question test that went with it about his likes and dislikes and so on. It was annoying, but when he started paying attention to the questions, he could understand where they came from and saw how the algorithm was going to work.

Programming had been what got him to where he was, as the CEO of his father's tech company, Arnoldson Robotics. Unlike many other parents, his father never guaranteed him a position and so he'd worked his way up from research and development to his current position at the top.

Once complete, the app told him to check back in two days to allow the system time to find a match. The last step was to tick a box if he wanted to be able to chat with dates once they were scheduled. Figuring why not, he ticked the box.

He laughed as he set his phone down. At the rate he was going, there wasn't going to be a match for him anywhere. People were interested in his name, the money, and the face that went with it, but few cared about him outside of that.

He stood, stretched, and headed for his bedroom. Tomorrow was Saturday and that meant no suits, which always made it worth getting through the week. It wasn't that he minded dressing the part in his fitted suits, but there was something to be said about jeans and a shirt and blending in.

He slid on sweats before crawling into his king-sized bed. His room was the only real pop of color in his apartment and no one ever saw it. He liked things simple and understated in his room. With the exception of the TV that was hidden in the wall behind a painting that slid out of the way with the touch of a button.

He yawned as he lay back, watching the ceiling fan spin. Tomorrow he was going to hit up the farmer's market and just enjoy not being the most popular man. Well, he was going to give it a shot, anyway.

With any luck, he might meet someone among the vendors and shoppers that didn't know who he was and didn't want anything from him. Then he could let this whole blind date thing go and not have to do it.

Dinner, in the dark, at a restaurant, what a wild concept. It was expensive too, he noted, and if he invited someone on a date, he had to pay, and vice versa. All in all, it was an interesting business concept, and he could see why Evan had been interested in it.

Also by Toni Denise

Learn More or get buy links for any of these books at my author website:

tonidenisebooks.com

Westbeach Series:

Old Friends

On the Run

One Last Chance

Out of Time

Series Boxset

Finding Love Series:

Engaged to Her Neighbor

Married to the Playboy

Falling for Her Fake Husband

Short and Steamy Duet:

The Wedding Date

The Wedding Ruse

Stone Twins Duet:

Please Stay

Don't Leave

(Don't Leave is included in the "Mine This Winter" collection available
Dec 1, 2022)

Billionaire Blind Dates:

Owen (this book)

Jake

Evan

Stand-alone:

Fighting Chance (Coming 2022)

Lightning Source UK Ltd.
Milton Keynes UK
UKHW010644051022
409964UK00001B/160

9 798201 910822